Reprint Publishing

FOR PEOPLE WHO GO FOR ORIGINALS.

www.reprintpublishing.com

[Page 8.

"'ARE YOU RELATED TO GOVERNOR McKINLEY?'"

COFFEE AND REPARTEE

BY

JOHN KENDRICK BANGS

ILLUSTRATED

NEW YORK AND LONDON

HARPER & BROTHERS PUBLISHERS

1899

TO

F. S. M.

ILLUSTRATIONS

I

THE guests at Mrs. Smithers's high-class boarding-house for gentlemen had assembled as usual for breakfast, and in a few moments Mary, the dainty waitress, entered with the steaming coffee, the mush, and the rolls.

The School-master, who, by-the-way, was suspected by Mrs. Smithers of having intentions, and who for that reason occupied the chair nearest the lady's heart, folded up the morning paper, and placing it under him so that no one else could get it, observed, quite genially for him, "It was very wet yesterday."

"I didn't find it so," observed a young man seated half-way down the table, who was by common consent called the Idiot, because of his "views." "In fact, I was very dry. Curious thing, I'm always dry on rainy days. I am one of the kind of men who know that it is the part of wisdom to stay in when it rains, or to carry an umbrella when it is not possible to stay at home, or, having no home, like ourselves, to remain cooped up in stalls, or stalled up in coops, as you may prefer."

"You carried an umbrella, then?" queried the landlady, ignoring the Idiot's shaft at the size of her "elegant and airy apartments with an ease born of experience.

"Yes, madame," returned the Idiot, quite unconscious of what was coming.

"Whose?" queried the lady, a sarcastic smile playing about her lips.

"That I cannot say, Mrs. Smithers," replied the Idiot, serenely, "but it is the one you usually carry."

"Your insinuation, sir," said the School-master, coming to the landlady's rescue, "is an unworthy one. The umbrella in question is mine. It has been in my possession for five years."

"Then," replied the Idiot, unabashed, "it is time you returned it. Don't you think men's morals are rather lax in this matter of umbrellas, Mr. Whitechoker?" he added, turning from the School-master, who began to show signs of irritation.

"Very," said the Minister, running his finger about his neck to make the collar which had been sent home from the laundry by mistake set more easily—"very lax. At the last Conference I attended, some person, forgetting his high office as a minister in the Church, walked off with my umbrella without so much as a thank you; and it was embarrassing too, because the rain was coming down in bucketfuls."

"What did you do?" asked the landlady, sympathetically. She liked Mr. Whitechoker's sermons, and, beyond this, he was a more profitable boarder than any of the others, remaining home to luncheon every day and having to pay extra therefor.

"There was but one thing left for me to do. I took the bishop's umbrella," said Mr. Whitechoker, blushing slightly.

"But you returned it, of course?" said the Idiot.

"I intended to, but I left it on the train on my way back home the next day," replied the clergyman, visibly embarrassed by the Idiot's unexpected cross-examination.

"It's the same way with books," put in the Biblicmaniac, an unfortunate being whose love of rare first editions had brought him down from affluence to boarding. "Many a man who wouldn't steal a dollar would run off with a book. I had a friend once who had a rare copy of *Through Africa by Daylight*. It was a beautiful book. Only twenty-five copies printed. The margins of the pages were four inches wide, and the title-page was rubricated; the frontispiece was colored by hand, and the seventeenth page had one of the most amusing typographical errors on it—"

"Was there any reading-matter in the book?" queried the Idiot, blowing softly on a hot potato that was nicely balanced on the end of his fork.

"Yes, a little; but it didn't amount to much," returned the Bibliomaniac. "But, you know, it isn't as reading-matter that men like myself care for books. We have a higher notion than that. It is as a specimen of book-making that we admire a chaste bit of literature like *Through Afri-*

"ALARMED THE COOK"

ca by Daylight. But, as I was saying, my friend had this book, and he'd extra-illustrated it. He had pictures from all parts of the world in it, and the book had grown from a volume of one hundred pages to four volumes of two hundred pages each."

"And it was stolen by a highly honorable friend, I suppose?" queried the Idiot.

"Yes, it was stolen—and my friend never knew by whom," said the Bibliomaniac.

"What?" asked the Idiot, in much surprise. "Did you never confess?"

It was very fortunate for the Idiot that the buckwheat cakes were brought on at this moment. Had there not been some diversion of that kind, it is certain that the Bibliomaniac would have assaulted him.

"It is very kind of Mrs. Smithers, I think," said the School-master, "to provide us with such delightful cakes as these free of charge."

"Yes," said the Idiot, helping himself to six cakes. "Very kind indeed, although I must say they are extremely economical from an architectural point of view—which is to say, they are rather fuller of pores than of buckwheat. I wonder why it is," he continued, possibly to avert the landlady's retaliatory comments—" I wonder why it is that porous plasters and buckwheat cakes are so similar in appearance ?"

" And so widely different in their respective effects on the system," put in a genial old gentleman who occasionally imbibed, seated next to the Idiot.

" I fail to see the similarity between a buckwheat cake and a porous plaster," said the School-master, resolved, if possible, to embarrass the Idiot.

" You don't, eh ?" replied the latter. " Then it is very plain, sir, that you have never eaten a porous plaster."

To this the School-master could find no reasonable reply, and he took refuge in silence. Mr. Whitechoker tried to look severe ; the gentleman who occasionally imbibed smiled all over; the Bibliomaniac ignored the remark entirely, not having as yet forgiven the Idiot for his gross insinuation regarding his friend's *édition de luxe* of *Through Africa by Daylight;* Mary, the maid, who greatly admired the Idiot, not so much for his idiocy as for the aristocratic manner in which he carried himself, and the

truly striking striped shirts he wore, left the
room in a convulsion of laughter that so
alarmed the cook below-stairs that the next
platterful of cakes were more like tin plates
than cakes; and as for Mrs. Smithers, that
worthy woman was speechless with wrath.
But she was not paralyzed apparently, for
reaching down into her pocket she brought
forth a small piece of paper, on which was
written in detail the "account due" of the
Idiot.

"I'd like to have this settled, sir," she
said, with some asperity.

"Certainly, my dear madame," replied
the Idiot, unabashed—"certainly. Can you
change a check for a hundred?"

No, Mrs. Smithers could not.

"Then I shall have to put off paying the
account until this evening," said the Idiot.
"But," he added, with a glance at the
amount of the bill, "are you related to
Governor McKinley, Mrs. Smithers?"

"I am not," she returned, sharply. "My
mother was a Partington."

"I only asked," said the Idiot, apologeti-
cally, "because I am very much interested
in the subject of heredity, and you may not

know it, but you and he have each a marked tendency towards high-tariff bills."

And before Mrs. Smithers could think of anything to say, the Idiot was on his way down town to help his employer lose money on Wall Street.

II

"Do you know, I sometimes think—" began the Idiot, opening and shutting the silver cover of his watch several times with a snap, with the probable, and not altogether laudable, purpose of calling his landlady's attention to the fact—of which she was already painfully aware—that breakfast was fifteen minutes late.

"Do you, really?" interrupted the Schoolmaster, looking up from his book with an air of mock surprise. "I am sure I never should have suspected it."

"Indeed?" returned the Idiot, undisturbed by this reflection upon his intellect. "I don't really know whether that is due to your generally unsuspicious nature, or to your shortcomings as a mind-reader."

"There are some minds," put in the landlady at this point, "that are so small that it would certainly ruin the eyes to read them."

"I have seen many such," observed the Idiot, suavely. "Even our friend the Bibliomaniac at times has seemed to me to be very absent-minded. And that reminds me, Doctor," he continued, addressing himself to the medical boarder. "What is the cause of absent-mindedness?"

"That," returned the Doctor, ponderously, "is a very large question. Absent-mindedness, generally speaking, is the result of the projection of the intellect into surroundings other than those which for want of a better term I might call the corporeally immediate."

"So I have understood," said the Idiot, approvingly. "And is absent-mindedness acquired or inherent?"

Here the Idiot appropriated the roll of his neighbor.

"That depends largely upon the case," replied the Doctor, nervously. "Some are born absent-minded, some achieve absent-mindedness, and some have absent-mindedness thrust upon them."

"As illustrations of which we might take, for instance, I suppose," said the Idiot, "the born idiot, the borrower, and the man who is knocked silly by the pole of a truck on Broadway."

"Precisely," replied the Doctor, glad to get out of the discussion so easily. He was a very young doctor, and not always sure of himself.

"Or," put in the School-master, "to condense our illustrations, if the Idiot would kindly go out upon Broadway and encounter the truck, we should find the three combined in him."

The landlady here laughed quite heartily, and handed the School-master an extra strong cup of coffee.

"There is a great deal in what you say," said the Idiot, without a tremor. "There are very few scientific phenomena that cannot be demonstrated in one way or another by my poor self. It is the exception always that proves the rule, and in my case you find a consistent converse exemplification of all three branches of absent-mindedness."

"He talks well," said the Bibliomaniac, *sotto voce*, to the Minister.

"Yes, especially when he gets hold of large words. I really believe he reads," replied Mr. Whitechoker.

"'WHAT ARE THE FIRST SYMPTOMS OF INSANITY?'"

"I know he does," said the School-master, who had overheard. "I saw him reading Webster's Dictionary last night. I have noticed, however, that generally his vocabulary is largely confined to words that come between the letters A and F, which shows that as yet he has not dipped very deeply into the book."

"What are you murmuring about?" queried the Idiot, noting the lowered tone of those on the other side of the table.

"We were conversing—ahem! about—" began the Minister, with a despairing glance at the Bibliomaniac.

"Let me say it," interrupted the Bibliomaniac. "You aren't used to prevarication, and that is what is demanded at this time. We were talking about—ah—about—er—"

"Tut! tut!" ejaculated the School-master. "We were only saying we thought the—er —the—that the—"

"What *are* the first symptoms of insanity, Doctor?" observed the Idiot, with a look of wonder at the three shuffling boarders opposite him, and turning anxiously to the physician.

"I wish you wouldn't talk shop," retorted

the Doctor, angrily.   Insanity was one of his weak points.

"It's a beastly habit," said the School-master, much relieved at this turn of the conversation.

"Well, perhaps you are right," returned the Idiot. "People do, as a rule, prefer to talk of things they know something about, and I don't blame you, Doctor, for wanting to keep out of a medical discussion. I only asked my last question because the behavior of the Bibliomaniac and Mr. Whitechoker and the School-master for some time past has worried me, and I didn't know but what you might work up a nice little practice among us. It might not pay, but you'd find the experience valuable, and I think unique."

"It is a fine thing to have a doctor right in the house," said Mr. Whitechoker, kindly, fearing that the Doctor's manifest indignation might get the better of him.

"That," returned the Idiot, "is an assertion, Mr. Whitechoker, that is both true and untrue. There are times when a physician is an ornament to a boarding-house; times when he is not. For instance, on

Wednesday morning if it had not been for the surgical skill of our friend here, our good landlady could never have managed properly to distribute the late autumn chicken we found upon the menu. Tally one for the affirmative. On the other hand, I must confess to considerable loss of appetite when I see the Doctor rolling his bread up into little pills, or measuring the vinegar he puts on his salad by means of a glass dropper, and taking the temperature of his coffee with his pocket thermometer. Nor do I like—and I should not have mentioned it save by way of illustrating my position in regard to Mr. Whitechoker's assertion— nor do I like the cold, eager glitter in the Doctor's eyes as he watches me consuming, with some difficulty, I admit, the cold pastry we have served up to us on Saturday mornings under the wholly transparent *alias* of 'Hot Bread.' I may have very bad taste, but, in my humble opinion, the man who talks shop is preferable to the one who suggests it in his eyes. Some more iced potatoes, Mary," he added, calmly.

"Madame," said the Doctor, turning angrily to the landlady, "this is insufferable.

" ' READING WEBSTER'S DICTIONARY ' "

You may make out my bill this morning. I shall have to seek a home elsewhere."

" Oh, now, Doctor !" began the landlady, in her most pleading tone.

" Jove !" ejaculated the Idiot. " That's a good idea, Doctor. I think I'll go with you ; I'm not altogether satisfied here myself, but to desert so charming a company as we have here had never occurred to me. Together, however, we can go forth, and perhaps find happiness. Shall we put on our hunting togs and chase the fiery, untamed hall-room to the death this morning, or shall we put it off until some pleasanter day ?"

" Put it off," observed the School-master, persuasively. " The Idiot was only indulging in persiflage, Doctor. That's all. When you have known him longer you will understand him better. Views are as necessary to him as sunlight to the flowers; and I truly think that in an asylum he would prove a delightful companion."

" There, Doctor," said the Idiot; " that's handsome of the School-master. He couldn't make more of an apology if he tried. I'll forgive him if you will. What say you ?"

And strange to say, the Doctor, in spite

of the indignation which still left a red tinge on his cheek, laughed aloud and was reconciled.

As for the School-master, he wanted to be angry, but he did not feel that he could afford his wrath, and for the first time in some months the guests went their several ways at peace with each other and the world.

III

THERE was a conspiracy in hand to embarrass the Idiot. The School-master and the Bibliomaniac had combined forces to give him a taste of his own medicine. The time had not yet arrived which showed the Idiot at a disadvantage; and the two boarders, the one proud of his learning, and the other not wholly unconscious of a bookish life, were distinctly tired of the triumphant manner in which the Idiot always left the breakfast-table to their invariable discomfiture.

It was the School-master's suggestion to put their tormentor into the pit he had heretofore digged for them. The worthy instructor of youth had of late come to see that while he was still a prime favorite with his landlady, he had, nevertheless, suffered somewhat in her estimation because of the apparent ease with which the Idiot had got the better of him on all points. It was necessary, he thought, to rehabilitate himself, and a deep-laid plot, to which the Bibliomaniac readily lent ear, was the result of his reflections. They twain were to indulge in a discussion of the great story of *Robert Elsmere*, which both were confident the Idiot had not read, and concerning which they felt assured he could not have an intelligent opinion if he had read it.

So it happened upon this bright Sunday morning that as the boarders sat them down to partake of the usual " restful breakfast," as the Idiot termed it, the Bibliomaniac observed :

" I have just finished reading *Robert Elsmere*."

" Have you, indeed ?" returned the Schoolmaster, with apparent interest. " I trust you profited by it ?"

" On the contrary," observed the Bibliomaniac. " My views are much unsettled by it."

" I prefer the breast of the chicken, Mrs. Smithers," observed the Idiot, sending his plate back to the presiding genius of the table. " The neck of a chicken is graceful. but not too full of sustenance."

" He fights shy," whispered the Bibliomaniac, gleefully.

" Never mind," returned the School-master, confidently; "we'll land him yet." Then
he added, aloud: "Unsettled by it? I
fail to see how any man with beliefs that
are at all the result of mature convictions
can be unsettled by the story of *Elsmere*.
For my part I believe, and I have always
said—"

" I never could understand why the neck
of a chicken should be allowed on a respec-
table table anyhow," continued the Idiot,
ignoring the controversy in which his neighbors were engaged, "unless for the purpose of showing that the deceased fowl met
with an accidental rather than a natural
death."

" In what way does the neck demonstrate
that point?" queried the Bibliomaniac, forgetting the conspiracy for a moment.

" By its twist or by its length, of course,"
returned the Idiot. " A chicken that dies a
natural death does not have its neck wrung;
nor when the head is removed by the use
of a hatchet, is it likely that it will be cut
off so close behind the ears that those who

"'I STUCK TO THE PIGS'"

eat the chicken are confronted with four inches of neck."

"Very entertaining indeed," interposed the School-master; "but we are wandering from the point the Bibliomaniac and I were discussing. Is or is not the story of *Robert Elsmere* unsettling to one's beliefs? Perhaps you can help us to decide that question."

"Perhaps I can," returned the Idiot; "and perhaps not. It did not unsettle my beliefs."

"But don't you think," observed the Bibliomaniac, "that to certain minds the book is more or less unsettling?"

"To that I can confidently say no. The certain mind knows no uncertainty," replied the Idiot, calmly.

"Very pretty indeed," said the School-master, coldly. "But what was your opinion of Mrs. Ward's handling of the subject? Do you think she was sufficiently realistic? And if so, and Elsmere weakened under the stress of circumstances, do you think—or don't you think—the production of such a book harmful, because—being real—it must of necessity be unsettling to some minds?"

THE CONSPIRATORS

"I prefer not to express an opinion on that subject," returned the Idiot, "because I never read *Robert Els—*"

"Never read it?" ejaculated the School-master, a look of triumph in his eyes.

"Why, everybody has read *Elsmere* that pretends to have read anything," asserted the Bibliomaniac.

"Of course," put in the landlady, with a scornful laugh.

"Well, I didn't," said the Idiot, non-chalantly. "The same ground was gone over two years before in Burrows's great story, *Is It, or Is It Not?* and anybody who ever read Clink's books on the *Non-Existent as Opposed to What Is*, knows where Burrows got his points. Burrows's story was a perfect marvel. I don't know how many editions it went through in England, and when it was translated into French by Madame Tournay, it simply set the French wild."

"Great Scott!" whispered the Bibliomaniac, desperately, "I'm afraid we've been barking up the wrong tree."

"You've read Clink, I suppose?" asked the Idiot, turning to the School-master.

"Y—yes," returned the School-master, blushing deeply.

The Idiot looked surprised, and tried to conceal a smile by sipping his coffee from a spoon.

"And Burrows?"

"No," returned the School-master, humbly. "I never read Burrows."

"Well, you ought to. It's a great book, and it's the one *Robert Elsmere* is taken from —same ideas all through, I'm told—that's why I didn't read *Elsmere*. Waste of time, you know. But you noticed yourself, I suppose, that Clink's ground is the same as that covered in *Elsmere?*"

"No; I only dipped lightly into Clink," returned the School-master, with some embarrassment.

"But you couldn't help noticing a similarity of ideas?" insisted the Idiot, calmly.

The School-master looked beseechingly at the Bibliomaniac, who would have been glad to fly to his co-conspirator's assistance had he known how, but never having heard of Clink, or Burrows either, for that matter, he made up his mind that it was best for his

reputation for him to stay out of the controversy.

"Very slight similarity, however," said
the School-master, in despair.

" Where can I find Clink's books?" put in
Mr. Whitechoker, very much interested.

The Idiot conveniently had his mouth
full of chicken at the moment, and it was
to the School-master who had also read
him that they all—the landlady included—
looked for an answer.

"Oh, I think," returned that worthy, hes-
itatingly—" I think you'll find Clink in any
of the public libraries."

" What is his full name?" persisted Mr.
Whitechoker, taking out a memorandum-
book.

" Horace J. Clink," said the Idiot.

" Yes ; that's it—Horace J. Clink," echoed
the School-master. " Very virile writer and
a clear thinker," he added, with some nerv-
ousness.

" What, if any, of his books would you
specially recommend?" asked the Minister
again.

The Idiot had by this time risen from
the table, and was leaving the room with

the genial gentleman who occasionally imbibed.

The School-master's reply was not audible.

" I say," said the genial gentleman to the
Idiot, as they passed out into the hall, " they
didn't get much the best of you in that matter.   But, tell me, who was Clink, anyhow?"

" Never heard of him before," returned
the Idiot.

" And Burrows?"

" Same as Clink."

" Know anything about *Elsmere?*" chuc-
kled the genial gentleman.

" Nothing—except that it and ' Pigs in
Clover' came out at the same time, and I
stuck to the Pigs."

And the genial gentleman who occasionally imbibed was so pleased at the plight of
the School-master and of the Bibliomaniac
that he invited the Idiot up to his room,
where the private stock was kept for just
such occasions, and they put in a very pleasant morning together.

IV

THE guests were assembled as usual. The oatmeal course had been eaten in silence. In the Idiot's eye there was a cold glitter of expectancy—a glitter that boded ill for the man who should challenge him to controversial combat—and there seemed also to be, judging from sundry winks passed over the table and kicks passed under it, an understanding to which he and the genial gentleman who occasionally imbibed were parties.

As the School-master sampled his coffee the genial gentleman who occasionally imbibed broke the silence.

"I missed you at the concert last night, Mr. Idiot," said he.

"Yes," said the Idiot, with a caressing movement of the hand over his upper lip; "I was very sorry, but I couldn't get around last night. I had an engagement with a number of friends at the athletic club. I meant to have dropped you a line in the afternoon telling you about it, but I forgot it until it was too late. Was the concert a success?"

"Very successful indeed. The best one, in fact, we have had this season, which makes me regret all the more deeply your absence," returned the genial gentleman, with a suggestion of a smile playing about his lips. "Indeed," he added, "it was the finest one I've ever seen."

"The finest one you've what?" queried the School-master, startled at the verb.

"The finest one I've ever seen," replied the genial gentleman. "There were only ten performers, and really, in all my experience as an attendant at concerts, I never saw such a magnificent rendering of Beethoven as we had last night. I wish you could have been there. It was a sight for the gods."

"I don't believe," said the Idiot, with a slight cough that may have been intended to conceal a laugh—and that may also have been the result of too many cigarettes—"I don't believe it could have been any more interesting than a game of pool I heard at the club."

"It appears to me," said the Bibliomaniac to the School-master, "that the popping sounds we heard late last night in the Idiot's room may have some connection with the present mode of speech these two gentlemen affect."

"Let's hear them out," returned the School-master, "and then we'll take them into camp, as the Idiot would say."

"I don't know about that," replied the genial gentleman. "I've seen a great many concerts, and I've heard a great many good games of pool, but the concert last night was simply a ravishing spectacle. We had a Cuban pianist there who played the orchestration of the first act of *Parsifal* with surprising agility. As far as I could see, he didn't miss a note, though it was a little annoying to observe how he used the pedals."

"Too forcibly, or how?" queried the Idiot.

"Not forcibly enough," returned the Imbiber. "He tried to work them both with one foot. It was the only thing to mar an otherwise marvellous performance. The idea of a man trying to display Wagner

"'WEREN'T YOUR EARS LONG ENOUGH?'"

with two hands and one foot is irritating to a musician with a trained eye."

"I wish the Doctor would come down," said Mrs. Smithers, anxiously.

"Yes," put in the School-master; "there seems to be madness in our midst."

"Well, what can you expect of a Cuban, anyhow?" queried the Idiot. "The Cuban, like the Spaniard or the Italian or the African, hasn't the vigor which is necessary for the proper comprehension and rendering of Wagner's music. He is by nature slow and indolent. If it were easier for a Spaniard to hop than to walk, he'd hop, and rest his other leg. I've known Italians whose diet was entirely confined to liquids, because they were too tired to masticate solids. It is the ease with which it can be absorbed that makes macaroni the favorite dish of the Italians, and the fondness of all Latin races for wines is entirely due, I think, to the fact that wine can be swallowed without chewing. This indolence affects also their language. The Italian and the Spaniard speak the language that comes easy— that is soft and dreamy; while the Germans and Russians, stronger, more energetic, indulge in a speech that even to us, who are people of an average amount of energy, is sometimes appalling in the severity of the strain it puts upon the tongue. So, while I do not wonder that your Cuban pianist showed woful defects in his use of the pedals, I do wonder that, even with his surprising agility, he had sufficient energy to manipulate the keys to the satisfaction of so competent a witness as yourself."

"It was too bad; but we made up for it later," asserted the other. "There was a young girl there who gave us some of Mendelssohn's Songs without Words. Her expression was simply perfect. I wouldn't have missed it for all the world; and now that I think of it, in a few days I can let you see for yourself how splendid it was. We persuaded her to encore the songs in the dark, and we got a flash-light photograph of two of them."

"Oh! then it was not on the piano-forte she gave them?" said the Idiot.

"Oh no; all labial," returned the genial gentleman.

Here Mr. Whitechoker began to look concerned, and whispered something to the

School-master, who replied that there were
enough others present to cope with the two
parties to the conversation in case of a vio-
lent outbreak.

" I'd be very glad to see the photographs,"
replied the Idiot. "Can't I secure copies of
them for my collection ? You know I have
the complete rendering of ' Home, Sweet
Home ' in kodak views, as sung by Patti.
They are simply wonderful, and they prove
what has repeatedly been said by critics,
that, in the matter of expression, the superior of Patti has never been seen."

" I'll try to get them for you, though I
doubt it can be done. The artist is a very
shy young girl, and does not care to have
her efforts given too great a publicity until
she is ready to go into music a little more
deeply. She is going to read the 'Moon-
light Sonata ' to us at our next concert.
You'd better come. I'm told her gestures
bring out the composer's meaning in a manner never as yet equalled."

" I'll be there; thank you," returned the
Idiot. " And the next time those fellows
at the club are down for a pool tournament
I want you to come up and hear them play.

"'THE CORKS POPPED TO SOME PURPOSE LAST NIGHT.'"

It was extraordinary last night to hear the balls dropping one by one — click, click, click — as regularly as a metronome, into the pockets. One of the finest shots, I am sorry to say, I missed."

"How did it happen?" asked the Bibliomaniac. "Weren't your ears long enough?"

"It was a kiss shot, and I couldn't hear it," returned the Idiot.

"I think you men are crazy," said the School-master, unable to contain himself any longer.

"So?" observed the Idiot, calmly. "And how do we show our insanity?"

"Seeing concerts and hearing games of pool."

"I take exception to your ruling," returned the Imbiber. "As my friend the Idiot has frequently remarked, you have the peculiarity of a great many men in your profession, who think because they never happened to see or do or hear things as other people do, they may not be seen, done, or heard at all. I *saw* the concert I attended last night. Our musical club has rooms next to a hospital, and we have to give silent concerts for fear of disturbing

the patients; but we are all musicians of
sufficient education to understand by a
glance of the eye what you would fail to
comprehend with fourteen ears and a mi-
crophone."

" Very well said," put in the Idiot, with a
scornful glance at the School-master. " And
I literally heard the pool tournament. I was
dining in a room off the billiard-hall, and
every shot that was made, with the exception of the one I spoke of, was distinctly
audible. You gentlemen, who think you
know it all, wouldn't be able to supply a
bureau of information at the rate of five
minutes a day for an hour on a holiday.
Let's go up-stairs," he added, turning to
the Imbiber, "where we may discuss our
last night's entertainment apart from this
atmosphere of rarefied learning. It makes
me faint."

And the Imbiber, who was with difficulty
keeping his lips in proper form, was glad
enough to accept the invitation. "The corks
popped to some purpose last night," he said,
later on.

" Yes," said the Idiot; " for a conspiracy
there's nothing so helpful as popping corks."

V

"WHEN you get through with the fire, Mr. Pedagog," observed the Idiot, one winter's morning, noticing that the ample proportions of the School-master served as a screen to shut off the heat from himself and the genial gentleman who occasionally imbibed, "I wish you would let us have a little of it. Indeed, if you could conveniently spare so little as one flame for my friend here and myself, we'd be much obliged."

"It won't hurt you to cool off a little, sir," returned the School-master, without moving.

"No, I am not so much afraid of the injury that may be mine as I am concerned for you. If that fire should melt our only refrigerating material, I do not know what our good landlady would do. Is it true, as the Bibliomaniac asserts, that Mrs. Smithers leaves all her milk and butter in your room overnight, relying upon your coolness to keep them fresh ?"

" I never made any such assertion," said the Bibliomaniac, warmly.

" I am not used to having my word disputed," returned the Idiot, with a wink at the genial old gentleman.

" But I never said it, and I defy you to prove that I said it," returned the Bibliomaniac, hotly.

" You forget, sir," said the Idiot, coolly, " that you are the one who disputes my assertion. That casts the burden of proof on your shoulders. Of course if you can prove that you never said anything of the sort, I withdraw; but if you cannot adduce proofs, you, having doubted my word, and publicly at that, need not feel hurt if I decline to accept all that you say as gospel."

" You show ridiculous heat," said the School-master.

" Thank you," returned the Idiot, gracefully. "And that brings us back to the original proposition that you would do well to show a little yourself."

" Good-morning, gentlemen," said Mrs.

Smithers, entering the room at this moment. "It's a bright, fresh morning."

"Like yourself," said the School-master, gallantly.

"Yes," added the Idiot, with a glance at the clock, which registered 8.45—forty-five minutes after the breakfast hour—"very like Mrs. Smithers—rather advanced."

To this the landlady paid no attention; but the School-master could not refrain from saying,

"Advanced, and therefore not backward, like some persons I might name."

"Very clever," retorted the Idiot, "and really worth rewarding. Mrs. Smithers, you ought to give Mr. Pedagog a receipt in full for the past six months."

"Mr. Pedagog," returned the landlady, severely, "is one of the gentlemen who always have their receipts for the past six months."

"Which betrays a very saving disposition," accorded the Idiot. "I wish I had all I'd received for six months. I'd be a rich man."

"Would you, now?" queried the Bibliomaniac. "That is interesting enough. How

"'IF YOU COULD SPARE SO LITTLE AS ONE FLAME'"

men's ideas differ on the subject of wealth!
Here is the Idiot would consider himself
rich with $150 in his pocket—"

"Do you think he gets as much as that?"
put in the School-master, viciously. "Five
dollars a week is rather high pay for one of
his—"

"Very high indeed," agreed the Idiot.
"I wish I got that much. I might be able
to hire a two-legged encyclopædia to tell
me everything, and have over $4.75 a week
left to spend on opera, dress, and the poor
but honest board Mrs. Smithers provides,
if my salary was up to the $5 mark; but
the trouble is men do not make the fabu-
lous fortunes nowadays with the ease with
which you, Mr. Pedagog, made yours. There
are, no doubt, more and greater opportuni-
ties to-day than there were in the olden
time, but there are also more men trying
to take advantage of them. Labor in the
business world is badly watered. The colleges are turning out more men in a week
nowadays than the whole country turned
out in a year forty years ago, and the quality is so poor that there has been a general
reduction of wages all along the line. Where

does the struggler for existence come in when he has to compete with the college-bred youth who, for fear of not getting employment anywhere, is willing to work for nothing? People are not willing to pay for what they can get for nothing."

"I am glad to hear from your lips so complete an admission," said the School-master, "that education is downing ignorance."

"I am glad to know of your gladness," returned the Idiot. "I didn't quite say that education was downing ignorance. I plead guilty to the charge of holding the belief that unskilled omniscience interferes very materially with skilled sciolism in skilled sciolism's efforts to make a living."

"Then you admit your own superficiality?" asked the School-master, somewhat surprised by the Idiot's command of syllables.

"I admit that I do not know it all," returned the Idiot. "I prefer to go through life feeling that there is yet something for me to learn. It seems to me far better to admit this voluntarily than to have it forced home upon me by circumstances, as happened in the case of a college graduate I know, who speculated on Wall Street, and lost the hundred dollars that were subsequently put to a good use by the uneducated me."

"From which you deduce that ignorance is better than education?" queried the School-master, scornfully.

"For an omniscient," returned the Idiot, "you are singularly near-sighted. I have made no such deduction. I arrive at the conclusion, however, that in the chase for the gilded shekel the education of experience is better than the coddling of Alma Mater. In the satisfaction—the personal satisfaction—one derives from a liberal education, I admit that the sons of Alma Mater are the better off. I never could hope to be so self-satisfied, for instance, as you are."

"No," observed the School-master, "you cannot raise grapes on a thistle farm. Any unbiassed observer looking around this table," he added, "and noting Mr. Whitechoker, a graduate of Yale; the Bibliomaniac, a son of dear old Harvard; the Doctor, an honor man of Williams; our legal friend here, a graduate of Columbia

THE SCHOOLMASTER AS A COOLER

—to say nothing of myself, who was graduated with honors at Amherst—any unbiassed observer seeing these, I say, and then seeing you, wouldn't take very long to make up his mind as to whether a man is better off or not for having had a collegiate training."

"There I must again dispute your assertion," returned the Idiot. " The unbiassed person of whom you speak would say, 'Here is this gray-haired Amherst man, this book-loving Cambridge boy of fifty-seven years of age, the reverend graduate of Yale, class of '55, and the other two learned gentlemen of forty-nine summers each, and this poor ignoramus of an Idiot, whose only virtue is his modesty, all in the same box.' And then he would ask himself, 'In what way have these sons of Amherst, Yale, Harvard, and so forth, the better of the unassuming Idiot?'"

"The same box?" said the Bibliomaniac. "What do you mean by that?"

"Just what I say," returned the Idiot. "The same box. All boarding, all eschewing luxuries of necessity, all paying their bills with difficulty, all sparsely clothed; in reality, all keeping Lent the year through. 'Verily,' he would say, 'the Idiot has the best of it, for he is young.'"

And leaving them chewing the cud of reflection, the Idiot departed.

"I thought they were going to land you that time," said the genial gentleman who occasionally imbibed, later; "but when I heard you use the word 'sciolism,' I knew you were all right. Where did you get it?"

"My chief got it off on me at the office the other day. I happened in a mad moment to try to unload some of my original observations on him apropos of my getting to the office two hours late, in which it was my endeavor to prove to him that the truly safe and conservative man was always slow, and so apt to turn up late on occasions. He hopped about the office for a minute or two, and then he informed me that I was an 18-karat sciolist. I didn't know what he meant, and so I looked it up."

"And what did he mean?"

"He meant that I took the cake for superficiality, and I guess he was right," replied the Idiot, with a smile that was not altogether mirthful.

4

VI

"GOOD-MORNING!" said the Idiot, cheerfully, as he entered the dining-room.

To this remark no one but the landlady vouchsafed a reply. "I don't think it is," she said, shortly. "It's raining too hard to be a very good morning."

"That reminds me," observed the Idiot, taking his seat and helping himself copiously to the hominy. "A friend of mine on one of the newspapers is preparing an article on the 'Antiquity of Modern Humor.' With your kind permission, Mrs. Smithers, I'll take down your remark and hand it over to Mr. Scribuler as a specimen of the modern antique joke. You may not be aware of the fact, but that jest is to be found in the rare first edition of the *Tales of Bobbo*, an Italian humorist, who stole everything he wrote from the Greeks."

"So?" queried the Bibliomaniac. "I never heard of Bobbo, though I had, before the

"'READING THE SUNDAY NEWSPAPERS'"

auction sale of my library, a choice copy of
the *Tales of Poggio*, bound in full crushed
Levant morocco, with gilt edges, and one
or two other Italian *Joe Millers* in tree calf.
I cannot at this moment recall their names."

"At what period did Bobbo live?" in-
quired the School-master.

"I don't exactly remember," returned
the Idiot, assisting the last potato on the
table over to his plate. "I don't know exactly. It was subsequent to B.C., I think,
although I may be wrong. If it was not,
you may rest assured it was prior to B.C."

"Do you happen to know," queried the
Bibliomaniac, "the exact date of this rare
first edition of which you speak?"

"No; no one knows that," returned the
Idiot. "And for a very good reason. It
was printed before dates were invented."

The silence which followed this bit of information from the Idiot was almost insult-
ing in its intensity. It was a silence that
spoke, and what it said was that the Idiot's
idiocy was colossal, and he, accepting the
stillness as a tribute, smiled sweetly.

"What do you think, Mr. Whitechoker,"
he said, when he thought the time was ripe

for renewing the conversation—"what do
you think of the doctrine that every day
will be Sunday by-and-by?"

"I have only to say, sir," returned the
Dominie, pouring a little hot water into his
milk, which was a bit too strong for him,
"that I am a firm believer in the occurrence
of a period when Sunday will be to all prac-
tical purposes perpetual."

"That is my belief, too," observed the
School-master. "But it will be ruinous to
our good landlady to provide us with one
of her exceptionally fine Sunday breakfasts
every morning."

"Thank you, Mr. Pedagog," returned
Mrs. Smithers, with a smile. "Can't I give
you another cup of coffee?"

"You may," returned the School-master,
pained at the lady's grammar, but too courteous to call attention to it save by the em-
phasis with which he spoke the word "may."

"That's one view to take of it," said the
Idiot. "But in case we got a Sunday
breakfast every day in the week, we, on the
other hand, would get approximately what
we pay for. You may fill my cup too, Mrs.
Smithers."

"The coffee is all gone," returned the landlady, with a snap.

"Then, Mary," said the Idiot, gracefully, turning to the maid, "you may give me a glass of ice-water. It is quite as warm, after all, as the coffee, and not quite so weak. A perpetual Sunday, though, would have its drawbacks," he added, unconscious of the venomous glances of the landlady. "You, Mr. Whitechoker, for instance, would be preaching all the time, and in consequence would soon break down. Then the effect upon our eyes from habitually reading the Sunday newspapers day after day would be extremely bad ; nor must we forget that an eternity of Sundays means the elimination from our midst,' as the novelists say, of baseball, of circuses, of horse-racing, and other necessities of life, unless we are prepared to cast over the Puritanical view of Sunday which now prevails. It would substitute Dr. Watts for 'Annie Rooney.' We should lose 'Ta-ra-ra-boom-de-ay' entirely, which is a point in its favor."

"I don't know about that," said the genial old gentleman. "I rather like that song."

"Did you ever hear me sing it?" asked the Idiot.

"Never mind," returned the genial old gentleman, hastily. "Perhaps you are right, after all."

The Idiot smiled, and resumed: "Our shops would be perpetually closed, and an enormous loss to the shopkeepers would be sure to follow. Mr. Pedagog's theory that we should have Sunday breakfasts every day is not tenable, for the reason that with a perpetual day of rest agriculture would die out, food products would be killed off

BOBBO

by unpulled weeds ; in fact, we should go back to that really unfortunate period when women were without dress-makers, and man's chief object in life was to christen animals as he met them, and to abstain from apples, wisdom, and full dress."

"The Idiot is right," said the Bibliomaniac. "It would not be a very good thing for the world if every day were Sunday. Wash-day is a necessity of life. I am willing to admit this, in the face of the fact that wash-day meals are invariably atrocious. Contracts would be void, as a rule, because Sunday is a *dies non*."

"A what?" asked the Idiot.

"A non-existent day in a business sense," put in the School-master.

"Of course," said the landlady, scornfully. "Any person who knows anything knows that."

"Then, madame," returned the Idiot, rising from his chair, and putting a handful of sweet crackers in his pocket—"then I must put in a claim for $104 from you, having been charged at the rate of one dollar a day for 104 *dies nons* in the two years I have been with you."

"Indeed!" returned the lady, sharply.
"Very well. And I shall put in a counter-
claim for the lunches you carry away from
breakfast every morning in your pockets."

"In that event we'll call it off, madame,"
returned the Idiot, as with a courtly bow
and a pleasant smile he left the room.

"Well, I call him 'off,'" was all the landlady could say, as the other guests took
their departure.

And of course the School-master agreed
with her.

VII

" OUR streets appear to be as far from perfect as ever," said the Bibliomaniac with a
sigh, as he looked out through the window
at the great pools of water that gathered in
the basins made by the sinking of the Belgian blocks. " We'd better go back to the
cowpaths of our fathers."

" There is a great deal in what you say,"
observed the School-master. " The cowpath has all the solidity of mother earth,
and none of the distracting noises we get
from the pavements that obtain to-day. It
is porous and absorbs the moisture. The
Belgian pavement is leaky, and lets it run
into our cellars. We might do far worse
than to go back—"

" Excuse me for having an opinion," said
the Idiot, " but the man of enterprise can't
afford to indulge in the luxury of the som-
nolent cowpath. It is too quiet. It con-
duces to sleep, which is a luxury business

men cannot afford to indulge in too freely. Man must be up and doing. The prosperity of a great city is to my mind directly due to its noise and clatter, which effectually put a stop to napping, and keep men at all times wide awake."

"This is a Welsh-rabbit idea, I fancy," said the School-master, quietly. He had overheard the Idiot's confidences, as revealed to the genial Imbiber, regarding the sources of some of his ideas.

"Not at all," returned the Idiot. "These ideas are beef—not Welsh-rabbit. They are the result of much thought. If you will put your mind on the subject, you will see for yourself that there is more in my theory than there is in yours. The prosperity of a locality is the greater as the noise in its vicinity increases. It is in the quiet neighborhood that man stagnates. Where do we find great business houses? Where do we find great fortunes made? Where do we find the busy bees who make the honey that enables posterity to get into Society and do nothing? Do we pick up our millions on the cowpath? I guess not. Do we erect our most princely business houses along the roads laid out by our bovine sister? I think not. Does the man who goes from the towpath to the White House take the short cut? I fancy not. He goes over the block pavement. He seeks the home of the noisy, clattering street before he lands in the shoes of Washington. The man who sticks to the cowpath may be able to drink milk, but he never wears diamonds."

"All that you say is very true, but it is not based on any fundamental principle. It is so because it happens to be so," returned the School - master. "If it were man's habit to have the streets laid out on the old cowpath principle in his cities he would be quite as energetic, quite as prosperous, as he is now."

"No fundamental principle involved? There is the fundamental principle of all business success involved," said the Idiot, warming up to his subject. "What is the basic quality in the good business man? Alertness. What is 'alertness?' Wide-awakeishness. In this town it is impossible for a man to sleep after a stated hour, and for no other reason than that the clatter of the pavements prevents him. As a

promoter of alertness, where is your cowpath? The cowpaths of the Catskills, and
we all know the mountains are riddled by
'em, didn't keep Rip Van Winkle awake,
and I'll wager Mr. Whitechoker here a
year's board that there isn't a man in his
congregation who can sleep a half-hour—
much less twenty years—with Broadway
within hearing distance.

"I tell you, Mr. Pedagog," he continued,
"it is the man from the cowpath who gets
buncoed. It's the man from the cowpath
who can't make a living even out of what
he calls his 'New York Store.' It is the
man from the cowpath who rejoices because he can sell ten dollars' worth of
sheep's-wool for five dollars, and is happy when he goes to meeting dressed up in a
four-dollar suit of clothes that has cost him
twenty."

"Your theory, my young friend," observed
the School-master, "is as fragile as this
cup"—tapping his coffee-cup. "The countryman of whom you speak is up and doing
long before you or I or your successful
merchant, who has waxed great on noise
as you put it, is awake. If the early bird

catches the worm, what becomes of your theory ?"

"The early bird does get the bait," replied the Idiot. "But he does not catch the fish, and I'll offer the board another wager that the Belgian block merchant is wider awake at 8 A.M., when he first opens his eyes, than his suburban brother who gets up at at five is all day. It's the extent to which the eyes are opened that counts, and as for your statement that the fact that prosperity and noisy streets go hand in hand is true only because it happens to be so, that is an argument which may be applied to any truth in existence. I am because I happen to be, not because I am. You are what you are because you are, because if you were not, you would not be what you are."

"Your logic is delightful," said the School-master, scornfully.

"I strive to please," replied the Idiot. "But I do agree with the Bibliomaniac that our streets are far from perfection," he added. "In my opinion they should be laid in strata. On the ground-floor should be the sewers and telegraph pipes; above this should be the water-mains, then a layer for trucks, then a broad stratum for carriages, above which should be a promenade for pedestrians. The promenade for pedestrians should be divided into four sections—one for persons of leisure, one for those in a hurry, one for peddlers, and one for beggars."

"Highly original," said the Bibliomaniac.

"And so cheap," added the School-master.

"In no part of the world," said the Idiot, in response to the last comment, "do we get something for nothing. Of course this scheme would be costly, but it would increase prosperity—"

"Ha! ha!" laughed the School-master, satirically.

"Laugh away, but you cannot gainsay my point. Our prosperity would increase, for we should not be always excavating to get at our pipes; our surface cars with a clear track would gain for us rapid transit, our truck-drivers would not be subjected to the temptations of stopping by the way-side to overturn a coupé, or to run down a pedestrian, our fine equipages would in consequence need fewer repairs, and as for the pedestrians, the beggars, if relegated to themselves, would be forced out of business as would also the street-peddlers. The men in a hurry would not be delayed by loungers, beggars, and peddlers, and the loungers would derive inestimable benefit from the arrangement in the saving of wear and tear on their clothes and minds by contact with the busy world."

"It would be delightful," acceded the School-master, "particularly on Sundays, when they were all loungers."

"Yes," replied the Idiot. "It would be delightful then, especially in summer, when covered with an awning to shield promenaders from the sun."

Mr. Pedagog sighed, and the Bibliomaniac, wearily declining a second cup of coffee, left the table with the Doctor, earnestly discussing with that worthy gentleman the causes of weakmindedness.

VlII

"THERE'S a friend of mine up near River-
dale," said the Idiot, as he unfolded his
napkin and let his bill flutter from it to the
floor, "who's tried to make a name for himself in literature."

"What's his name?" asked the Bibliomaniac, interested at once.

"That's just the trouble. He hasn't made
it yet," replied the Idiot. "He hasn't suc-
ceeded in his courtship of the Muse, and
beyond himself and a few friends his name
is utterly unknown."

"What work has he tried?" queried the
School-master, pouring unadmonished two
portions of skimmed milk over his oatmeal.

"A little of everything. First he wrote a
novel. It had an immense circulation, and
he only lost $300 on it. All of his friends
took a copy—I've got one that he gave me
—and I believe two hundred newspapers

were fortunate enough to secure the book for review. His father bought two, and tried to obtain the balance of the edition, but didn't have enough money. That was gratifying, but gratification is more apt to deplete than to strengthen a bank account."

"I had not expected so extraordinarily wise an observation from one so unusually unwise," said the School-master, coldly.

"Thank you," returned the Idiot. "But I think your remark is rather contradictory. You would naturally expect wise observations from the unusually unwise; that is, if your teaching that the expression ' unusually unwise' is but another form of the expression 'usually wise' is correct. But, as I was saying, when the genial instructor of youth interrupted me with his flattery," continued the Idiot, "gratification is gratifying but not filling, so my friend concluded that he had better give up novel-writing and try jokes. He kept at that a year, and managed to clear his postage-stamps. His jokes were good, but too classic for the tastes of the editors. Editors are peculiar. They have no respect for age—particularly in the matter of jests. Some of my friend's

WOOING THE MUSE

jokes had seemed good enough for Plutarch to print when he had a publisher at his mercy, but they didn't seem to suit the high and mighty products of this age who sit in judgment on such things in the comic-paper offices. So he gave up jokes."

"Does he still know you?" asked the landlady.

"Yes, madame," observed the Idiot.

"Then he hasn't given up all jokes," she retorted, with fine scorn.

"Tee-he-hee!" laughed the School-master. "Pretty good, Mrs. Smithers—pretty good."

"Yes," said the Idiot. "That is good, and, by Jove! it differs from your butter, Mrs. Smithers, because it's entirely fresh. It's good enough to print, and I don't think the butter is."

"What did your friend do next?" asked Mr. Whitechoker.

"He was employed by a funeral director in Philadelphia to write obituary verses for memorial cards."

"And was he successful?"

"For a time; but he lost his position because of an error made by a careless compositor in a marble‑yard. He had written,

> "' Here lies the hero of a hundred fights—
> Approximated he a perfect man;
> He fought for country and his country's rights,
> And in the hottest battles led the van.'"

"Fine in sentiment and in execution!" observed Mr. Whitechoker.

"Truly so," returned the Idiot. "But when the compositor in the marble‑yard got it engraved on the monument, my friend was away, and when the army post that was to pay the bill received the monument, the quatrain read,

> "' Here lies the hero of a hundred flights—
> Approximated he a perfect one;
> He fought his country and his country's rights,
> And in the hottest battles led the run.'"

"Awful!" ejaculated the Minister.

"Dreadful!" said the landlady, forgetting to be sarcastic.

"What happened?" asked the School‑master.

"He was bounced, of course, without a cent of pay, and the company failed the next week, so he couldn't make anything by suing for what they owed him."

"Mighty hard luck," said the Bibliomaniac.

"Very; but there was one bright side to the case," observed the Idiot. "He managed to sell both versions of the quatrain afterwards for five dollars. He sold the original one to a religious weekly for a dollar, and got four dollars for the other one from a comic paper. Then he wrote an anecdote about the whole thing for a Sunday newspaper, and got three dollars more out of it."

"And what is your friend doing now?" asked the Doctor.

"Oh, he's making a mint of money now, but no name."

"In literature?"

"Yes. He writes advertisements on salary," returned the Idiot. "He is writing now a recommendation of tooth-powder in Indian dialect."

"Why didn't he try writing an epic?" said the Bibliomaniac.

"Because," replied the Idiot, "the one aim of his life has been to be original, and

"HE GAVE UP JOKES"

he couldn't reconcile that with epic po.
etry."

At which remark the landlady stooped
over, and recovering the Idiot's bill from
under the table, called the maid, and osten-
tatiously requested her to hand it to the Idiot. He, taking a cigarette from his pocket,
thanked the maid for the attention, and rolling the slip into a taper, thoughtfully stuck
one end of it into the alcohol light under
the coffee-pot, and lighting the cigarette
with it, walked nonchalantly from the room.

IX

" I'VE just been reading a book," began the Idiot.

" I thought you looked rather pale," said the School-master.

" Yes," returned the Idiot, cheerfully, " it made me feel pale. It was about the pleasures of country life; and when I contrasted rural blessedness as it was there depicted with urban life as we live it, I felt as if my youth were being thrown away. I still feel as if I were wasting my sweetness on the desert air."

" Why don't you move?" queried the Bibliomaniac, suggestively.

" If I were purely selfish I should do so at once, but I am, like my good friend Mr. Whitechoker, a slave to duty. I deem it my duty to stay here to keep the School-master fully informed in the various branches of knowledge which are day by day opened up, many of which seem to be so

far beyond the reach of one of his conservative habits; to assist Mr. Whitechoker in
his crusades against vice at this table and
elsewhere; to give the Bibliomaniac the
benefit of my advice in regard to those pre-
cious little tomes he no longer buys—to
make life worth the living for all of you, to
say nothing of enabling Mrs. Smithers to
keep up the extraordinarily high standard
of this house by means of the hard-earned
stipend I pay to her every Monday morning."

"Every Monday?" queried the School-
master.

"Every Monday," returned the Idiot.
"That is, of course, every Monday that I
pay. The things one gets to eat in the
country, the air one breathes, the utter
freedom from restraint, the thousand and
more things one enjoys in the suburbs that
are not attainable here—it is these that
make my heart yearn for the open."

"Well, it's all rot," said the School-master, impatiently. "Country life is ideal
only in books. Books do not tell of running for trains through blinding snow-
storms; writers do not expatiate on the

"'A LITTLE GARDEN OF MY OWN, WHERE I COULD RAISE
AN OCCASIONAL CAN OF TOMATOES'"

delights of waking on cold winter nights and finding your piano and parlor furniture afloat because of bursted pipes, with the plumber, like Sheridan at Winchester, twenty miles away. They are dumb on the subject of the ecstasy one feels when pushing a twenty-pound lawn-mower up and down a weed patch at the end of a wearisome hot summer's day. They are silent—"

" Don't get excited, Mr. Pedagog, please," interrupted the Idiot. " I am not contemplating leaving you and Mrs. Smithers, but I do pine for a little garden of my own, where I could raise an occasional can of tomatoes. I dream sometimes of getting milk fresh from the pump, instead of twenty-four hours after it has been drawn, as we do here. In my musings it seems to me to be almost idyllic to have known a spring chicken in his infancy; to have watched a hind-quarter of lamb gambolling about its native heath before its muscles became adamant, and before chopped-up celery tops steeped in vinegar were poured upon it in the hope of hypnotizing boarders into the belief that spring lamb and mint-sauce lay before them. What care I how hard it is to rise every morning before six in winter to thaw out the boiler, so long as the night coming finds me seated in the genial glow of the gas log! What man is he that would complain of having to bale out his cellar every week, if, on the other hand, that cellar gains thereby a fertility that keeps its floor sheeny, soft, and green — an interior tennis-court — from spring to spring, causing the gladsome click of the lawn-mower to be heard within its walls all through the still watches of

"'A HIND-QUARTER OF LAMB GAMBOLLING ABOUT ITS NATIVE HEATH'"

the winter day? I tell you, sir, it is the life to lead, that of our rural brother. I do not believe that in this whole vast city there is a cellar like that—an in-door garden-patch, as it were."

"No," returned the Doctor; "and it is a good thing there isn't. There is enough sickness in the world without bringing any of your *rus* ideas *in urbe*. I've lived in the country, sir, and I assure you it is not what it is written up to be. Country life is misery, melancholy, and malaria."

"You must have struck a profitable section, Doctor," returned the Idiot, taking possession of three steaming buckwheat cakes to the dismay of Mr. Whitechoker, who was about to reach out for them himself. "And I should have supposed that your good business sense would have restrained you from leaving."

"Then the countryman is poor—always poor," continued the Doctor, ignoring the Idiot's sarcastic comments.

"Ah! that accounts for it," observed the Idiot. "I see why you did not stay; for what shall it profit a man to save a patient if practice, like virtue, is to be its own reward?"

"Your suggestion, sir," retorted the Doctor, "betrays an unhealthy frame of mind."

"That's all right, Doctor," returned the Idiot; "but please do not diagnose the case any further. I can't afford an expert opinion as to my mental condition. But to return to our subject: you two gentlemen appear to have had unhappy experiences in country life—quite different from those of a friend of mine who owns a farm. He doesn't have to run for trains; he is independent of plumbers, because the only pipes in his house are for smoking purposes. The farm produces corn enough to keep his family supplied all the year round and to sell a balance at a profit. Oats and wheat are harvested to an extent which keeps the cattle and declares dividends besides. He never suffers from the cold or heat. He is never afraid of losing his house or barns by fire, because the whole fire department of the neighboring village is, to a man, in love with the house-keeper's daughter, and is always on hand in force. The chickens are the envy and pride of the county, and there are so many of them that they have to take turns in going to roost. The pigs are the most intelligent of their kind, and are so happy they never grunt. In fact, everything is lovely and cheap, the only thing that hangs high being the goose."

"'THE GLADSOME CLICK OF THE LAWN-MOWER'"

"Quite an ideal, no doubt," put in the School-master, scornfully. "I suppose his is one of those model farms with steam-pipes under the walks to melt the snow in winter, and of course there is a vein of coal growing right up into his furnace ready to be lit."

"Yes," observed the Bibliomaniac; "and no doubt the chickens lay eggs in every style—poached, fried, scrambled, and boiled. The weeds in the garden grow so fast, I suppose, that they pull themselves up by the roots; and if there is anything left undone at the end of the day I presume tramps in dress suits, and courtly in manner, spring out of the ground and finish up for him."

"I'll bet he's not on good terms with his neighbors if he has everything you speak of in such perfection. These farmers get frightfully jealous of each other," asserted the Doctor, with a positiveness that seemed to be born of experience.

"He never quarrelled with one of them in his life," returned the Idiot. "He doesn't know them well enough to quarrel with them; in fact, I doubt if he ever sees them at all. He's very exclusive."

"Of course he is a born farmer to get everything the way he has it," suggested Mrs. Smithers.

"No, he isn't. He's a broker," said the

Idiot. "and a very successful one. I see him on the street every day."

"Does he employ a man to run the farm?" asked the Clergyman.

"No," returned the Idiot, "he has too much sense and too few dollars to do any such foolish thing as that."

"It must be one of those self-winding stock farms," put in the School-master, scornfully. "But I don't see how he can be a successful broker and make money off his farm at the same time. Your statements do not agree, either. You said he never had to run for trains."

"Well, he never has," returned the Idiot, calmly. "He never goes near his farm. He doesn't have to. It's leased to the husband of the house-keeper whose daughter has a crush on the fire department. He takes his pay in produce, and gets more than if he took it in cash on the basis of the New York vegetable market."

"Then you have got us into an argument about country life that ends—" began the School-master, indignantly.

"That ends where it leaves off," retorted the Idiot, departing with a smile on his lips.

" He's an Idiot from Idaho," asserted the Bibliomaniac.

" Yes; but I'm afraid idiocy is a little contagious," observed the Doctor, with a grin and sidelong glance at the Schoolmaster.

X

"Good-morning, gentlemen," said the Idiot, as he seated himself at the breakfast-table and glanced over his mail.

"Good-morning yourself," returned the Poet. "You have an unusually large number of letters this morning. All checks, I hope?"

"Yes," replied the Idiot. "All checks of one kind or another. Mostly checks on ambition—otherwise, rejections from my friends the editors."

"You don't mean to say that you write for the papers?" put in the School-master, with an incredulous smile.

"I try to," returned the Idiot, meekly. "If the papers don't take 'em, I find them useful in curing my genial friend who imbibes of insomnia."

"What do you write—advertisements?" queried the Bibliomaniac.

"No. Advertisement writing is an art to

which I dare not aspire. It's too great a tax on the brain," replied the Idiot.

"Tax on what?" asked the Doctor. He was going to squelch the Idiot.

"The brain," returned the latter, not ready to be squelched. "It's a little thing people use to think with, Doctor. I'd advise you to get one." Then he added, "I write poems and foreign letters mostly."

"I did not know that you had ever been abroad," said the clergyman.

"'YOU DON'T MEAN TO SAY THAT YOU WRITE FOR THE PAPERS?'"

"I never have," returned the Idiot.

"Then how, may I ask," said Mr. White-choker, severely, "how can you write foreign letters?"

"With my stub pen, of course," replied the Idiot. "How did you suppose—with an oyster-knife?"

The clergyman sighed.

"I should like to hear some of your poems," said the Poet.

"Very well," returned the Idiot. "Here's one that has just returned from the *Bengal Monthly*. It's about a writer who died some years ago. Shakespeare's his name. You've heard of Shakespeare, haven't you, Mr. Pedagog?" he added.

Then, as there was no answer, he read the verse, which was as follows:

SETTLED.

Yes! Shakespeare wrote the plays—'tis clear to me.
Lord Bacon's claim's condemned before the bar.
He'd not have penned, "what fools these mortals be!"
But—more correct—"what fools these mortals are!"

"That's not bad," said the Poet.

"Thanks," returned the Idiot. "I wish you were an editor. I wrote that last spring,

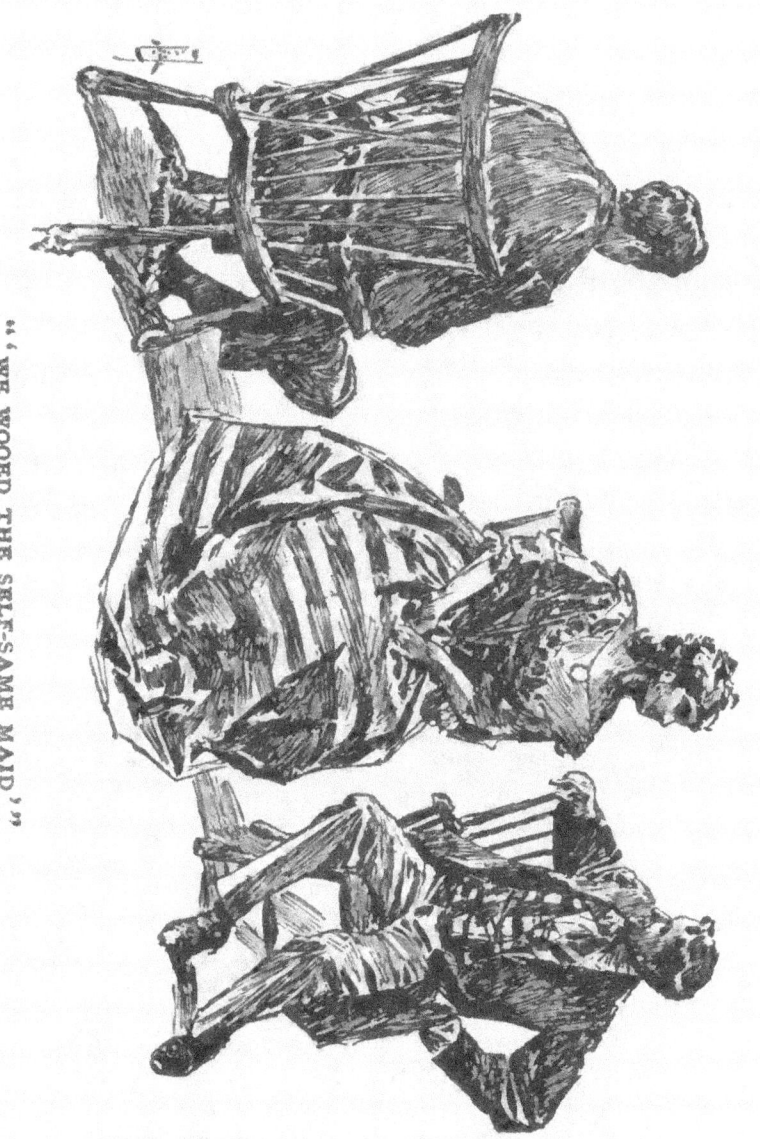

" ' WE WOOED THE SELF-SAME MAID ' "

and it has been coming back to me at the rate of once a week ever since."

"It is too short," said the Bibliomaniac.

"It's an epigram," said the Idiot. "How many yards long do you think epigrams should be ?"

The Bibliomaniac scorned to reply.

"I agree with the Bibliomaniac," said the School-master. "It is too short. People want greater quantity."

"Well, here is quantity for you," said the Idiot. "Quantity as she is not wanted by nine comic papers I wot of. This poem is called :

"'THE TURNING OF THE WORM.

"'How hard my fate perhaps you'll gather in,
  My dearest reader, when I tell you that
I entered into this fair world a twin—
  The one was spare enough, the other fat.

"'I was, of course, the lean one of the two,
  The homelier as well, and consequently
In ecstasy o'er Jim my parents flew,
  And good of me was spoken accident'ly.

"'As boys we went to school, and Jim, of course,
  Was e'er his teacher's favorite, and ranked
Among the lads renowned for moral force,
  Whilst I was every day right soundly spanked.

" ' Jim had an angel face, but there he stopped.
    I never knew a lad who'd sin so oft
And look so like a branch of heaven lopped
    From off the parent trunk that grows aloft.

" ' I seemed an imp—indeed 'twas often said
    That I resembled much Beelzebub.
My face was freckled and my hair was red—
    The kind of looking boy that men call scrub.

" ' Kind deeds, however, were my constant thought;
    In everything I did the best I could;
I said my prayers thrice daily, and I sought
    In all my ways to do the right and good.

" ' On Saturdays I'd do my Monday's sums,
    While Jim would spend the day in search of fun;
He'd sneak away and steal the neighbors' plums,
    And, strange to say, to earth was never run.

" ' Whilst I, when study-time was haply through,
    Would seek my brother in the neighbor's orchard;
Would find the neighbor there with anger blue,
    And as the thieving culprit would be tortured.

" ' The sums I'd done he'd steal, this lad forsaken,
    Then change my work, so that a paltry four
Would be my mark, whilst he had overtaken
    The maximum and all the prizes bore.

" ' In later years we loved the self-same maid;
    We sent her little presents, sweets, bouquets,
For which, alas! 'twas I that always paid;
    And Jim the maid now honors and obeys.

" ' We entered politics—in different roles,
    And for a minor office each did run.

'Twas I was left—left badly at the polls,
Because of fishy things that Jim had done.

"'When Jim went into business and failed,
I signed his notes and freed him from the strife
Which bankruptcy and ruin hath entailed
On them that lead a queer financial life.

"'Then, penniless, I learned that Jim had set
Aside before his failure—hard to tell!—
A half a million dollars on his pet—
His Mrs. Jim—the former lovely Nell.

"'That wearied me of Jim. It may be right
For one to bear another's cross, but I
Quite fail to see it in its proper light,
If that's the rule man should be guided by.

"'And since a fate perverse has had the wit
To mix us up so that the one's deserts
Upon the shoulders of the other sit,
No matter how the other one it hurts,

"'I am resolved to take some mortal's life;
Just when, or where, or how, I do not reck,
So long as law will end this horrid strife
And twist my dear twin brother's sinful neck.'"

"There," said the Idiot, putting down the manuscript. "How's that?"

"I don't like it," said Mr. Whitechoker. "It is immoral and vindictive. You should accept the hardships of life, no matter how

CURING INSOMNIA

unjust. The conclusion of your poem horrifies me, sir. I—"

" Have you tried your hand at dialect poetry ?" asked the Doctor.

" Yes; once," said the Idiot. " I sent it to the *Great Western Weekly*. Oh yes. Here it is. Sent back with thanks. It's an octette written in cigar-box dialect."

" In wh-a-at ?" asked the Poet.

" Cigar-box dialect. Here it is :

> " ' O Manuel garcia alonzo,
>   Colorado especial H. Clay,
> Invincible flora alphonzo,
>   Cigarette panatella el rey,
> Victoria Reina selectas—
>   O twofer madura grandé—
> O conchas oscuro perfectas,
>   You drive all my sorrows away.' "

" Ingenious, but vicious," said the Schoolmaster, who does not smoke.

" Again thanks. How is this for a sonnet ?" said the Idiot :

> " ' When to the sessions of sweet silent thought
>   I summon up remembrance of things past,
>   I sigh the lack of many a thing I sought,
>   And with old woes new wail my dear time's waste :
>   Then can I drown an eye, unused to flow,
>   For precious friends hid in death's dateless night,

And weep afresh love's long since cancel'd woe,
And moan the expense of many a vanish'd sight:
Then can I grieve at grievances foregone,
And heavily from woe to woe tell o'er
The sad account of fore-bemoaned moan,
Which I now pay as if not paid before.
But if the while I think of thee, dear friend!
All losses are restored and sorrows end.' "

" It is bosh !" said the School-master.

The Poet smiled quietly.

" Perfect bosh !" repeated the School-master. " And only shows how in weak hands so beautiful a thing as the sonnet can be made ridiculous."

"What's wrong with it ?" asked the Idiot.

" It doesn't contain any thought—or if it does, no one can tell what the thought is. Your rhymes are atrocious. Your phraseology is ridiculous. The whole thing is bad. You'll never get anybody to print it."

" I do not intend to try," said the Idiot, meekly.

" You are wise," said the School-master, " to take my advice for once."

" No, it is not your advice that restrains me," said the Idiot, dryly. " It is the fact that this sonnet has already been printed."

"In the name of Letters, where?" cried the School-master.

"In the collected works of William Shakespeare," replied the Idiot, quietly.

The Poet laughed; Mrs. Smithers's eyes filled with tears; and the School-master for once had absolutely nothing to say.

XI

"Do you believe, Mr. Whitechoker," said the Idiot, taking his place at the table, and holding his plate up to the light, apparently to see whether or not it was immaculate, whereat the landlady sniffed contemptuously—"do you believe that the love of money is the root of all evil?"

"I have always been of that impression," returned Mr. Whitechoker, pleasantly. "In fact, I am sure of it," he added. "There is no evil thing in this world, sir, that cannot be traced back to a point where greed is found to be its main-spring and the source of its strength."

"Then how do you reconcile this with the scriptural story of the forbidden fruit? Do you think the apples referred to were figures of speech, the true import of which was that Adam and Eve had their eyes on the original surplus?"

"Well, of course, there you begin to—

ah—you seem to me to be going back to the—er—the—ah—"

"Original root of all evil," prompted the Idiot, calmly.

"Precisely," returned Mr. Whitechoker, with a sigh of relief. "Mrs. Smithers, I think I'll have a dash of hot-water in my coffee this morning." Then, with a nervous glance towards the Idiot, he added, addressing the Bibliomaniac, "I think it looks like rain."

"Referring to the coffee, Mr. Whitechoker?" queried the Idiot, not disposed to let go of his victim quite so easily.

"Ah—I don't quite follow you," replied the Minister, with some annoyance.

"You said something looked like rain, and I asked you if the thing you referred to was the coffee, for I was disposed to agree with you," said the Idiot.

"I am sure," put in Mrs. Smithers, "that a gentleman of Mr. Whitechoker's refinement would not make any such insinuation, sir. He is not the man to quarrel with what is set before him."

"I ask your pardon, madam," returned the Idiot, politely. "I hope that I am not

"HOLDING HIS PLATE UP TO THE LIGHT"

the man to quarrel with my food, either.
Indeed, I make it a rule to avoid unpleas-
antness of all sorts, particularly with the
weak, under which category we find your
coffee. I simply wish to know to what Mr.
Whitechoker refers when he says 'it looks
like rain.'"

"I mean, of course," said the Minister,
with as much calmness as he could command—and that was not much—"I mean
the day. The day looks as if it might be
rainy."

"Any one with a modicum of brain knows
what you meant, Mr. Whitechoker," volun-
teered the School-master.

"Certainly," observed the Idiot, scraping
the butter from his toast; "but to those
who have more than a modicum of brains
my reverend friend's remark was not entirely clear. If I am talking of cotton, and
a gentleman chooses to state that it looks
like snow, I know exactly what he means.
He doesn't mean that the day looks like
snow, however; he refers to the cotton.
Mr. Whitechoker, talking about coffee,
chooses to state that it looks like rain,
which it undoubtedly does. I, realizing

that, as Mrs. Smithers says, it is not the gentleman's habit to attack too violently the food which is set before him, manifest some surprise, and, giving the gentleman the benefit of the doubt, afford him an opportunity to set himself right."

"Change the subject," said the Bibliomaniac, curtly.

"With pleasure," answered the Idiot, filling his glass with cream. "We'll change the subject, or the object, or anything you choose. We'll have another breakfast, or another variety of biscuits *frappé*—anything, in short, to keep peace at the table. Tell me, Mr. Pedagog," he added, "is the use of the word ' it,' in the sentence ' it looks like rain,' perfectly correct ?"

"I don't know why it is not," returned the School-master, uneasily. He was not at all desirous of parleying with the Idiot.

"And is it correct to suppose that ' it' refers to the day—is the day supposed to look like rain ?—or do we simply use ' it ' to express a condition which confronts us ?"

"It refers to the latter, of course."

"Then the full text of Mr. Whitechoker's remark is, I suppose, that ' the rainy condition of the atmosphere which confronts us looks like rain?'"

"Oh, I suppose so," sighed the School-master, wearily.

"Rather an unnecessary sort of statement that!" continued the Idiot. "It's something like asserting that a man looks like himself, or, as in the case of a child's primer—

"'See the cat?'

"'Yes, I see the cat.'

"'What is the cat?'"

"'The cat is a cat. Scat cat!'"

At this even Mrs. Smithers smiled.

"I don't agree with Mr. Pedagog," put in the Bibliomaniac, after a pause.

Here the School-master shook his head warningly at the Bibliomaniac, as if to indicate that he was not in good form.

"So I observe," remarked the Idiot. "You have upset him completely. See how Mr. Pedagog trembles?" he added, addressing the genial gentleman who occasionally imbibed.

"I don't mean that way," sneered the Bibliomaniac, bound to set Mr. Whitechoker straight. "I mean that the word 'it,' as em-

" ' I BELIEVE YOU'D BLOW OUT THE GAS IN YOUR
BED-ROOM ' "

ployed in that sentence, stands for day. The day looks like rain."

"Did you ever see a day?" queried the Idiot.

"Certainly I have," returned the Bibliomaniac.

"What does it look like?" was the calmly put question.

The Bibliomaniac's impatience was here almost too great for safety, and the manner in which his face colored aroused considerable interest in the breast of the Doctor, who was a good deal of a specialist in apoplexy.

"Was it a whole day you saw, or only a half-day?" persisted the Idiot.

"You may think you are very funny," retorted the Bibliomaniac. "I think you are—"

"Now don't get angry," returned the Idiot. "There are two or three things I do not know, and I'm anxious to learn. I'd like to know how a day looks to one to whom it is a visible object. If it is visible, is it tangible? and, if so, how does it feel?"

"The visible is always tangible," asserted the School-master, recklessly.

"How about a red - hot stove, or manifest indignation, or a view from a mountain-
top, or, as in the case of the young man in
the novel who 'suddenly waked,' and, 'looking anxiously about him, saw no one?'" returned the Idiot, imperturbably.

"Tut!" ejaculated the Bibliomaniac. "If
I had brains like yours, I'd blow them out."

"Yes, I think you would," observed the
Idiot, folding up his napkin. "You're just
the man to do a thing like that. I believe
you'd blow out the gas in your bedroom
if there wasn't a sign over it requesting
you not to." And filling his match - box
from the landlady's mantel supply, the Idiot
hurried from the room, and soon after left
the house.

XII

"IF my father hadn't met with reverses—"
the Idiot began.

"Did you really have a father?" interrupted the School-master. "I thought you were
one of these self-made Idiots. How terri-
ble it must be for a man to think that he is
responsible for you!"

"Yes," rejoined the Idiot; "my father
finds it rather hard to stand up under his
responsibility for me; but he is a brave old
gentleman, and he manages to bear the burden very well with the aid of my mother—
for I have a mother, too, Mr. Pedagog. A
womanly mother she is, too, with all the natural follies, such as fondness for and belief in
her boy. Why, it would soften your heart
to see how she looks on me. She thinks I
am the most everlastingly brilliant man she
ever knew—excepting father, of course, who
has always been a hero of heroes in her eyes,
because he never rails at misfortune, never

"'HIS FAIRY STORIES WERE TOLD HIM IN WORDS OF TEN SYLLABLES'"

spoke an unkind word to her in his life, and just lives gently along and waiting for the end of all things."

"Do you think it is right in you to deceive your mother in this way—making her think you a young Napoleon of intellect when you know you are an Idiot?" observed the Bibliomaniac, with a twinkle in his eye.

"Why certainly I do," returned the Idiot, calmly. "It's my place to make the old folks happy if I can; and if thinking me nineteen different kinds of a genius is going to fill my mother's heart with happiness, I'm going to let her think it. What's the use of destroying other people's idols even if we do know them to be hollow mockeries? Do you think you do a praiseworthy act, for instance, when you kick over the heathen's stone gods and leave him without any at all? You may not have noticed it, but I have—that it is easier to pull down an idol than it is to rear an ideal. I have had idols shattered myself, and I haven't found that the pedestals they used to occupy have been rented since. They are there yet and empty—standing as monuments to what once seemed good to me—and I'm no happier not no better for being disillusioned. So it is with my mother. I let her go on and think me perfect. It does her good, and it does me good because it makes me try to live up to that idea of hers as to what I am. If she had the same opinion of me that we all have she'd be the most miserable woman in the world."

"We don't all think so badly of you," said the Doctor, rather softened by the Idiot's remarks.

"No," put in the Bibliomaniac. "You are all right. You breathe normally, and you have nice blue eyes. You are graceful and pleasant to look upon, and if you'd been born dumb we'd esteem you very highly. It is only your manners and your theories that we don't like; but even in these we are disposed to believe that you are a well-meaning child."

"That is precisely the way to put it," assented the School-master. "You are harmless even when most annoying. For my own part, I think the most objectionable feature about you is that you suffer from that unfortunately not uncommon malady, extreme youth. You are young for your age, and if you only wouldn't talk, I think we should get on famously together."

"You overwhelm me with your compliments," said the Idiot. "I am sorry I am so young, but I cannot be brought to believe that that is my own fault. One must live to attain age, and how the deuce can one live when one boards?"

As no one ventured to reply to this question, the force of which very evidently, however, was fully appreciated by Mrs. Smithers, the Idiot continued:

"Youth is thrust upon us in our infancy, and must be endured until such a time as Fate permits us to account ourselves cured. It swoops down upon us when we have neither the strength nor the brains to resent it. Of course there are some superior persons in this world who never were young. Mr. Pedagog, I doubt not, was ushered into this world with all three sets of teeth cut, and not wailing as most infants are, but discussing the most abstruse philosophical problems. His fairy stories were told him, if ever, in words of ten syllables; and his father's first remark to him was doubtless an inquiry as to his opinion on the subject of

"'I THOUGHT MY FATHER A MEAN-SPIRITED ASSASSIN'"

Latin and Greek in our colleges. It's all right to be this kind of a baby if you like that sort of thing. For my part, I rejoice to think that there was once a day when I thought my father a mean-spirited assassin, because he wouldn't tie a string to the moon and let me make it rise and set as suited my sweet will. Babies of Mr. Pedagog's sort are fortunately like angel's visits, few and far between. In spite of his stand in the matter, though, I can't help thinking there was a great deal of truth in a rhyme a friend of mine got off on Youth. It fits the case. He said:

> " ' Youth is a state of being we attain
> In early years; to some 'tis but a crime—
> And, like the mumps, most agèd men complain,
> It can't be caught, alas! a second time.' "

"Your rhymes are interesting, and your reasoning, as usual, is faulty," said the School-master. " I passed a very pleasant childhood, though it was a childhood devoted, as you have insinuated, to serious rather than to flippant pursuits. I wasn't particularly fond of tag and hide-and-seek, nor do I think that even as an infant I ever cried for the moon."

"It would have expanded your chest if you had, Mr. Pedagog," observed the Idiot, quietly.

"So it would, but I never found myself short-winded, sir," retorted the School-master, with some acerbity.

"That is evident; but go on," said the Idiot. "You never passed a childish youth nor a youthful childhood, and therefore what?"

"Therefore, in my present condition, I am normally contented. I have no youthful follies to look back upon, no indiscretions to regret; I never knowingly told a lie, and—"

"All of which proves that you never were young," put in the Idiot; "and you will excuse me if I say it, but my father is the model for me rather than so exalted a personage as yourself. He is still young, though turned seventy, and I don't believe on his own account there ever was a boy who played hookey more, who prevaricated oftener, who purloined others' fruits with greater frequency than he. He was guilty of every crime in the calendar of youth; and if there is one thing that delights him more than another, it is to sit on a winter's night before the crackling log and tell us yarns about his youthful follies and his boyhood indiscretions."

"But is he normally a happy man?" queried the School-master.

"No."

"Ah!"

"No. He's an *ab*normally happy man, because he's got his follies and indiscretions to look back upon and not forward to."

"Ahem!" said Mrs. Smithers.

"Dear me!" ejaculated Mr. Whitechoker.

Mr. Pedagog said nothing, and the breakfast-room was soon deserted.

XIII

THERE was an air of suppressed excitement about Mrs. Smithers and Mr. Pedagog as they sat down to breakfast. Something had happened, but just what that something was no one as yet knew, although the genial old gentleman had a sort of notion as to what it was.

"Pedagog has been good-natured enough for an engaged man for nearly a week now," he whispered to the Idiot, who had asked him what he supposed was up, "and I have a half idea that Mrs. S. has at last brought him to the point of proposing."

"It's the other way, I imagine," returned the Idiot.

"You don't really think she has rejected him, do you?" queried the genial old gentleman.

"Oh no; not by a great deal. I mean that I think it very likely that he has brought her to the point. This is leap-year, you know," said the Idiot.

"Well, if I were a betting man, which I haven't been since night before last, I'd lay you a wager that they're engaged," said the old gentleman.

"I'm glad you've given up betting," rejoined the Idiot, "because I'm sure I'd take the bet if you offered it—and then I believe I'd lose."

"We are to have Philadelphia spring chickens this morning, gentlemen," said Mrs. Smithers, beaming upon all at the table. "It's a special treat."

"Which we all appreciate, my dear Mrs. Smithers," observed the Idiot, with a courteous bow to his landlady. "And, by the way, why is it that Philadelphia spring chickens do not appear until autumn, do you suppose? Is it because Philadelphia spring doesn't come around until it is autumn everywhere else?"

"No, I think not," said the Doctor. "I think it is because Philadelphia spring chickens are not sufficiently hardened to be able to stand the strain of exportation much before September, or else Philadelphia people do not get so sated with such delicacies as to permit any of the crop to go into other

" ' MRS. S. BROUGHT HIM TO THE POINT OF PROPOSING ' ".

than Philadelphia markets before that period. For my part, I simply love them."

"So do I," said the Idiot; "and if Mrs. Smithers will pardon me for expressing a preference for any especial part of the *pièce de résistance*, I will state to her that if, in helping me, she will give me two drumsticks, a pair of second joints, and plenty of the white meat, I shall be very happy."

"You ought to have said so yesterday," said the School-master, with a surprisingly genial laugh. "Then Mrs. Smithers could have prepared an individual chicken for you."

"That would be too much," returned the Idiot, "and I should really hesitate to eat too much spring chicken. I never did it in my life, and don't know what the effect would be. Would it be harmful, Doctor?"

"I really do not know how it would be," answered the Doctor. "In all my wide experience I have never found a case of the kind."

"It's very rarely that one gets too much spring chicken," said Mr. Whitechoker. "I haven't had any experience with patients, as my friend the Doctor has; but I have lived in many boarding-houses, and I have never yet known of any one even getting enough."

"Well, perhaps we shall have all we want this morning," said Mrs. Smithers. "I hope so, at any rate, for I wish this day to be a memorable one in our house. Mr. Pedagog has something to tell you. John, will you announce it now?"

"Did you hear that?" whispered the Idiot. "She called him 'John.'"

"Yes," said the genial old gentleman. "I didn't know Pedagog had a first name before."

"Certainly, my dear—that is, my very dear Mrs. Smithers," stammered the School-master, getting red in the face. "The fact is, gentlemen—ahem!—I—er—we—er—that is, of course—er—Mrs. Smithers has er—ahem! —Mrs. Smithers has asked me to be her— I — er — I should say I have asked Mrs. Smithers to be my husb — my wife, and— er—she—"

"Hoorah!" cried the Idiot, jumping up from the table and grasping Mr. Pedagog by the hand. "Hoorah! You've got in ahead of us, old man, but we are just as glad when we think of your good-fortune. Your gain may be our loss—but what of that where the happiness of our dear land-lady is at stake ?"

Mrs. Smithers glanced coyly at the Idiot and smiled.

" Thank you," said the School-master.

"You are welcome," said the Idiot. " Mrs. Smithers, you will also permit me to felicitate you upon this happy event. I, who have so often differed with Mr. Pedagog upon matters of human knowledge, am forced to admit that upon this occasion he has shown such eminently good sense that you are fortunate, indeed, to have won him."

" Again I thank you," said the School-master. " You are a very sensible person yourself, my dear Idiot ; perhaps my failure to appreciate you at times in the past has been due to your brilliant qualities, which have so dazzled me that I have been unable to see you as you really are."

" Here are the chickens," said Mrs. Smithers.

" Ah !" ejaculated the Idiot. " What lucky fellows we are, to be sure ! I hope, Mrs. Smithers, now that Mr. Pedagog has

"HOORAH!" CRIED THE IDIOT, GRASPING MR. PEDAGOG BY
THE HAND"

cut us all out, you will at least be a sister to the rest of us, and let us live at home."

"There is to be no change," said Mrs. Smithers—"at least, I hope not, except that Mr. Pedagog will take a more active part in the management of our home."

"I don't envy him that," said the Idiot. "We shall be severe critics, and it will be hard work for him to manage affairs better than you did, Mrs. Smithers."

"Mary, get me a larger cup for the Idiot's coffee," said Mrs. Smithers.

"Let's all retire from business," suggested the Idiot, after the other guests had expressed their satisfaction with the turn affairs had taken. "Let's retire from business, and change the Smithers Home for Boarders into an Educational Institution."

"For what purpose?" queried the Bibliomaniac.

"Everything is so lovely now," explained the Idiot, "that I feel as though I never wanted to leave the house again, even to win a fortune. If we turn it into a college and instruct youth, we need never go outside the front door excepting for pleasure."

"Where will the money and the instructors come from?" asked Mr. Whitechoker.

"Money? From pupils; and after we get going maybe somebody will endow us. As for instructors, I think we know enough to be instructors ourselves," replied the Idiot. "For instance: Pedagog's University. John Pedagog, President; Alonzo B. Whitechoker, Chaplain; Mrs. Smithers-Pedagog, Matron. For Professor of Belles - lettres, the Bibliomaniac, assisted by the Poet; Medical Lectures by Dr. Capsule; Chemistry taught by our genial friend who occasionally imbibes; Chair in General Information, your humble servant. Why, we would be overrun with pupils and money in less than a year."

"A very good idea," returned Mr. Pedagog. "I have often thought that a nice little school could be started here to advantage, though I must confess that I had different ideas on the subject of the instructors. You, my dear Idiot, would be a great deal more useful as a Professor Emeritus."

"Hm!" said the Idiot. "It sounds mighty

well—I've no doubt I should like it. What is a Professor Emeritus, Mr. Pedagog?"

"He is a professor who is paid a salary for doing nothing."

The whole table joined in a laugh, the Idiot included.

"By Jove! Mr. Pedagog," he said, as soon as he could speak, "you are just dead right about that. That's the place of places for me. Salary and nothing to do! Oh, how I'd love it!"

The rest of the breakfast was eaten in silence. The spring chickens were too good and too plentiful to admit of much waste of time in conversation. At the conclusion of the meal the Idiot rose from the table, and, after again congratulating Mr. Pedagog and his fiancée, announced that he was going to see his employer.

"On Sunday?" queried Mrs. Smithers.

"Yes; I want him to write me a recommendation as a man who can do nothing beautifully."

"And why, pray?" asked Mr. Pedagog.

"I'm going to apply to the Trustees of Columbia College the first thing to-morrow morning for an Emeritus Professorship, for if anybody can do nothing and draw money for it gracefully I'm the man. Wall Street is too wearing on my nerves," he replied.

And in a moment he was gone.

" I *like* him," said Mrs. Smithers.

" So do I," said Mr. Pedagog. He isn't half the idiot he thinks he is."

THE END

Reprint Publishing

FOR PEOPLE WHO GO FOR ORIGINALS.

This book is a facsimile reprint of the original edition. The term refers to the facsimile with an original in size and design exactly matching simulation as photographic or scanned reproduction.

Facsimile editions offer us the chance to join in the library of historical, cultural and scientific history of mankind, and to rediscover.

The books of the facsimile edition may have marks, notations and other marginalia and pages with errors contained in the original volume. These traces of the past refers to the historical journey that has covered the book.

ISBN 978-3-95940-057-2

www.reprintpublishing.com